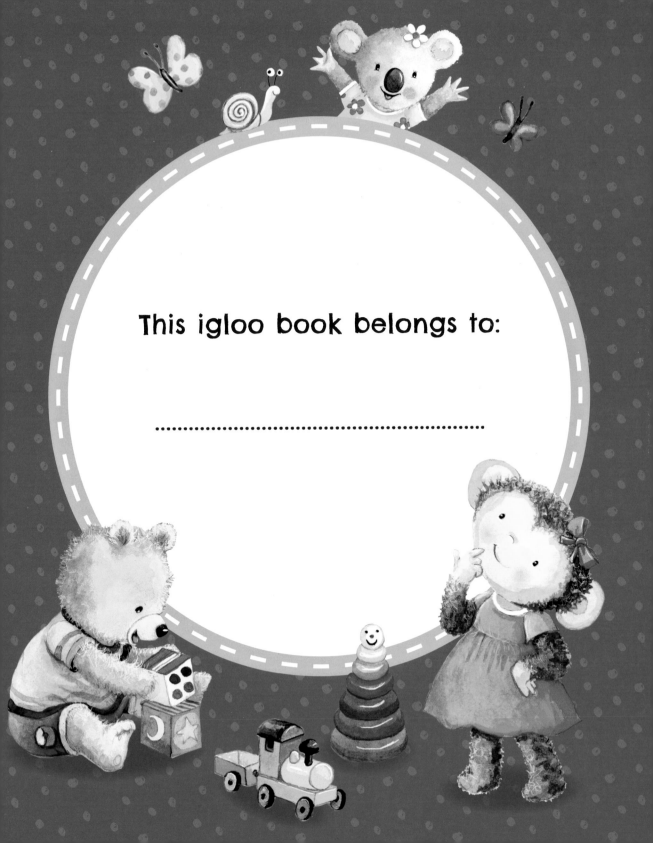

This igloo book belongs to:

....

Contents

igloobooks

Published in 2018
by Igloo Books Ltd, Cottage Farm, Sywell, NN6 0BJ
www.igloobooks.com

Copyright © 2017 Igloo Books Ltd

Written by Melanie Joyce
Illustrated by Gail Yerrill

Designed by Kerri-Ann Hulme
Edited by Caroline Richards

WKT001 0818
2 4 6 8 10 9 7 5 3
ISBN 978-1-78670-692-8

Printed and manufactured in China

Stories for

1

Year Olds

igloobooks

It's Playtime!

Boom, boom!

goes Leo's drum.

It's time for **noisy** playtime fun.

5

Here is Blue Train racing round.
Nelly makes a **woo-woo** sound.

Conny giggles. She says,

Toby sits by Tilly's side.

They're going on a ride!

George loves to...

... jump
and
Play.

He's having lots of fun today.

Oh, **look,** here comes Jack.

He's got drinks and some snacks.

It's time for a picnic in the sun.

Noisy playtime is so much **fun!**

You and Me

You and me **love** to play,
on a warm and sunny day.

We **giggle** and go outside.

I count and you hide.

Behind the tree...

... and plant
pots, too.

I look **everywhere** for you.

You aren't hiding
in the shed...

... or among the flowerbed.

I look and search around.
Then I hear a little **sound**.

It's a **snuffle** and a **giggle.**

I see two **eyes...**

... and a cute nose **wiggle.**

I creep up very quietly to you.

Then I say,

Found you.
Boo!

20

I kiss you and hug you **tight.**
You **squeal** with delight.

21

We play **again** and I don't mind,
that you hide and I find.

We **love** to play together.
The fun we have will last **forever**.

Bonny Loves

Bonny **loves** the morning sun,
waking up to have some **fun**.

She **loves** a hug from Mummy...

... and **breakfast** in her tummy.

Bonny **loves** to be outside.

Sliding on her yellow slide.

On the swing,
beneath the tree.

Bonny swings,

one,

two,

three.

Bonny **loves** to laugh and play.

Bouncing **up** and **down** all day.

Mummy sings a lullaby.
Humming bees go **buzzing** by.

Bonny **loves** to snooze and nap.

Curled up in her mummy's lap.

Bonny **loves** to wake and then,
playtime starts all over **again!**

Barney's Bedtime

Barney, please put your toys away,

said Mummy at the end of the day.

It was time to go to bed,
but Barney wanted to **play** instead.

33

Barney scooped up all his toys.
He made a lot of **noise.**

Barney said,

I play.
Toys play,
too!

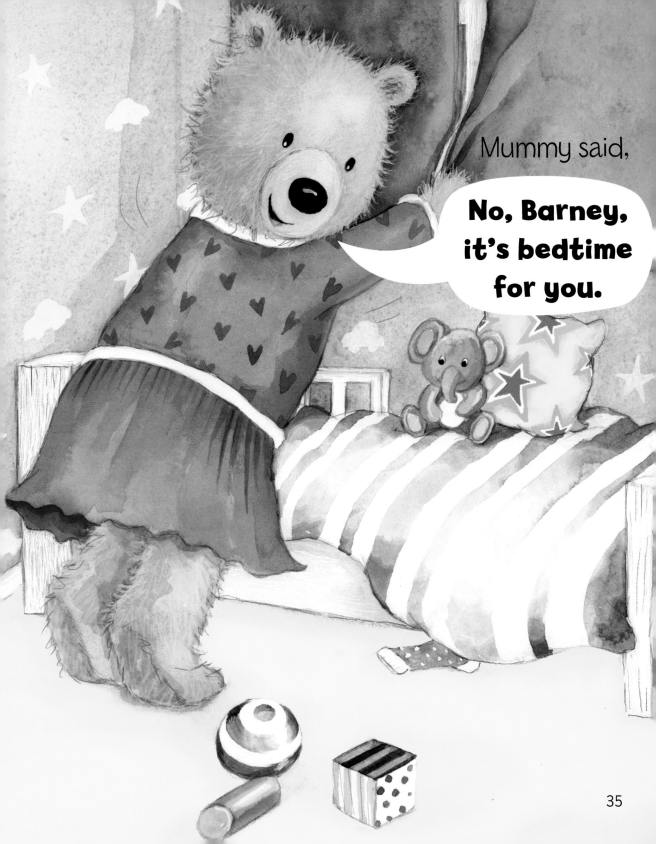

Mummy said,

No, Barney, it's bedtime for you.

Mummy said,

No more play.

But **naughty** Barney
just ran away.

Barney giggled. This was **fun.**

He just wanted to **run** and **run.**

So Barney ran round,
very fast.

Mummy knew it
wouldn't last.

Soon, Barney **flumped** down in a heap.

He was ready to go to sleep.

Mummy smiled and said,

**There, there.
Time for bed,
my little bear.**

Night, Night

One round moon shining bright.

Hoo-hoo,

says the owl
at night.

Up the stairs, sleepy head.
Time to get ready for bed.

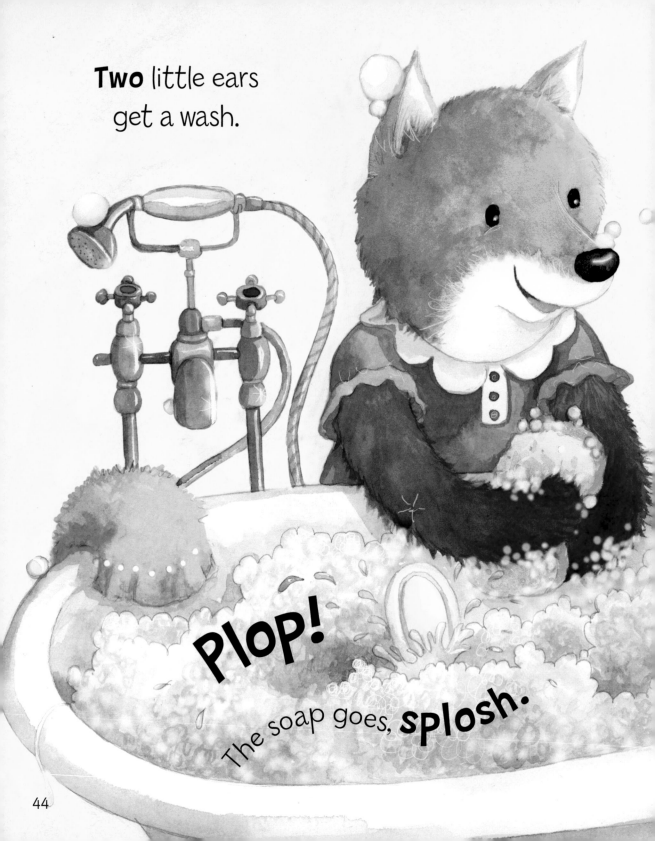

Two little ears
get a wash.

Plop!

The soap goes, **splosh.**

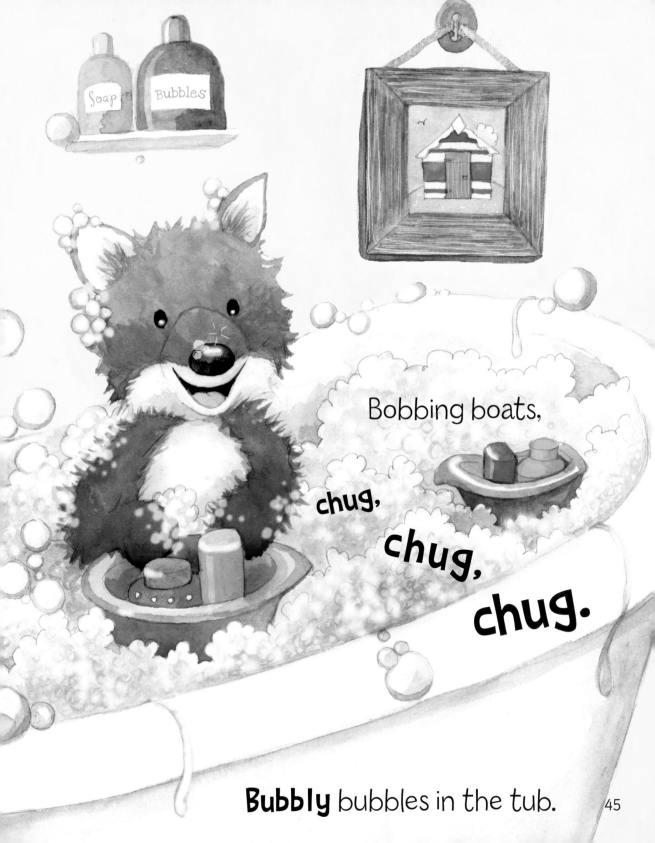

Bobbing boats,

chug,

chug,

chug.

Bubbly bubbles in the tub. 45

Three stories in a book.
Open it, let's take a look.

Four kisses just for you.

Even one for **Teddy**, too.

Five stars twinkling above.

Goodnight, my little love.